to the little brown blob under the chair,
who's actually not so little
and not really brown
and maybe not even much of a blob

Farrar Straus Giroux Books for Young Readers
175 Fifth Avenue, New York 10010

Copyright © 2014 by Gabi Swiatkowska
Color separations by Bright Arts (H.K.) Ltd.
Printed in China by Toppan Leefung Printing Ltd.,
Dongguan City, Guangdong Province
First edition, 2014
10 9 8 7 6 5 4 3 2 1

mackids.com

Library of Congress Cataloging-in-Publication Data
Swiatkowska, Gabi, author, illustrator.
    Queen on Wednesday / Gabi Swiatkowska. — First edition.
      pages cm
    Summary: When Thelma is bored, she decides to become a queen but the
responsibilities are so great that she soon has a royal headache.
    ISBN 978-0-374-37446-4 (hardcover)
    [1. Kings, queens, rulers, etc.—Fiction.] I. Title.

PZ7.S9755Que 2014
[E]—dc23

2013019719

Farrar Straus Giroux Books for Young Readers may be purchased for business or promotional
use. For information on bulk purchases please contact Macmillan Corporate and Premium
Sales Department at (800) 221-7945 x5442 or by email at specialmarkets@macmillan.com.

Queen on Wednesday

Gabi Swiatkowska

FRANCES FOSTER BOOKS

FARRAR STRAUS GIROUX

New York

On

Wednesday,

Thelma

was

bored.

Nothing had

happened

since Sunday.

So...

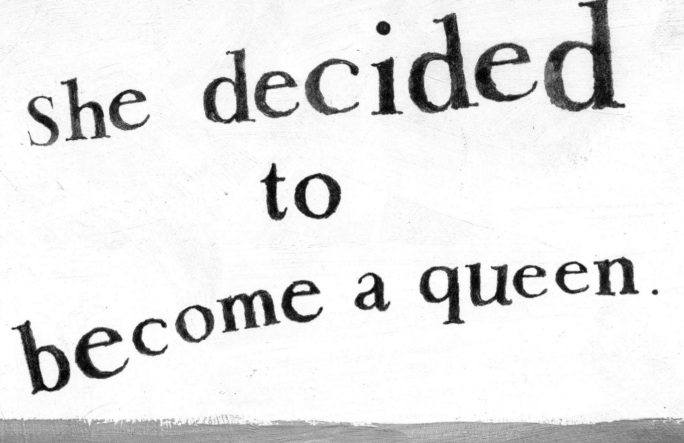

She decided
to
become a queen.

Of course,

she had to make
an announcement.

so on Thursday,

things
definitely livened up.

Friday Was very exciting.

Thelma had to choose the royal pets

and sit for a royal photograph.

The royal gown proved very useful in the rain.

or
two,

or
three—

because my dear children, imagination is one of the most fun and precious things

and a carriage that

could
hold **them** all.

On Saturday, Thelma went
in search of a proper castle.

She soon realized she simply
had to find
a maid and an animal
trainer.

Of course, they would have to be

royally qualified.

On Sunday,
Thelma
was
feeling faint.
She didn't
know
why.

Then she remembered:

they didn't have a royal cook.

On Monday, Thelma had to find

an electrician,

a veterinarian,

a plumber,

and a nurse.

She had a royal headache.

On
Tuesday,

it dawned on Thelma
they were
short on beds.

"That's it!" she cried.
She flung off
her royal crown
and
stomped away.

On Wednesday,
Thelma was bored.